The Strict Notary

A SHORT & SMUTTY SPANKING ROMANCE

ANNIKA STOUT

Annika Stout
ORCA - Calle Gil-Vernet 54/55
Les Tapies 1 #1087
Hospitalet de l'Infant, Tarragona 43890
Spain
https://annikastout.com

The Strict Notary

Contents

To Kathia

It's time to change your notary…

Chapter One

The rock shot through the air. Noelia stopped running abruptly and watched the stone fly in slow motion towards the fancy car.

Nooooooooooooo!

There was no possibility of avoiding the impact on the car, parked at the side of the road.

Closing her eyes only intensified the sound of the rock hitting metal.

Fuuuuuuuuuuck!

When she opened her eyes again, she saw a deep dent in the car. The white lacquer was chipped away.

Noelia froze when she realized someone was sitting in the car.

Any chance of flight - vanished.

Her heart stopped when the driver's door opened and a man dressed in an expensive-looking suit got out of the car. And he didn't look happy at all.

"I'm so sorry, it was an accident!"

"Is this what people do in the suburbs?" he asked. "Throw rocks at cars?"

Noelia's eyes widened and she had to remember to close her mouth.

Wow, he's one of those, she thought.

Obviously, he thought he was something better than people who lived in the suburbs.

"I didn't *throw* a rock. I kicked it accidentally while I was running."

"Running? You call that slow trot running? At that pace, it should be quite simple to look where you're stepping and not kick rocks around like a five-year-old!"

Noelia couldn't believe this guy. Determined not to let him intimidate her, she put her hands on her hips. It was time for the best teacher in town to give him one of her famous lectures.

"Running is about much more than speed. Running is about discipline. The thing that gets you out of the house no matter what temperature, if you feel like it or not, if you have sore legs or not. Clocking mile after mile without finding any excuses."

Take that Mr. Smartass, she thought.

He laughed out loud.

"Are you seriously laughing at me?" Noelia couldn't believe it.

"Discipline?" he asked. "Really?"

"Yes. Discipline. Any problem with that?"

Her patience was about to run out and that meant a lot, as she considered herself a very patient person. You had to be when you were surrounded all day long by teenagers.

Noelia hated people who thought they belonged to a superior species. Money didn't make you better or smarter. If anything, it just made people arrogant. This guy was a 100% purebred snob with his stupid fancy car.

His eyes were fixated on her.

"What you are describing is called perseverance. Discipline is something else," he said.

"Oh really, why don't you spit out your fancy definition then? Please, I'm all ears."

He stepped closer, towering over her. She had to admit that whatever fancy cologne he used, it smelled really good.

"Discipline is," he explained, looking into her eyes, "if I would take you over my knee right now and give you a sound spanking for kicking a rock at my car and then talking down to me."

Did he really just threaten me with a spanking? she wondered.

Despite all her willpower, it was impossible not to get aroused by his words but she couldn't let him see her weakness.

"Me? Talking down to you? You're the snob here talking down to me!"

Totally ignoring her, he took out his phone and started taking pictures of the damaged spot on the car.

"I will send the photos to my garage for an estimate. Maybe you should call your insurance to find out if they need an official accident report."

Insurance?

Noelia hated it when her parents were right. They always preached how liability insurance was the number one insurance to have.

"It doesn't matter, I don't have insurance," she said.

When Noelia started to run, she instantly regretted her decision to let him follow her to her house. He had offered her a ride in his fancy schmancy car, but she'd politely declined.

At least her parents could be proud of her for listening to them about never getting into the car with a stranger. Instead, she now had him staring and surely judging her ass for the next ten minutes while driving right behind her.

She ran faster than usual.

Slow trot? Kicking rocks like a five-year-old?

His mocking voice and stupid comments echoed in her head.

. . .

Arriving at the house, Noelia fetched her ID and phone. Passing by the mirror she saw her red face.

Ugh!

He was perfectly put together and smelled amazing and she was in her running gear, red like a tomato, and started smelling sweaty. It couldn't get much worse.

"I will have you contacted when I get the quote from the garage," he said after taking pictures of her ID and saving her phone number. "In case you need to contact me, here's my business card."

As soon as she took his card, he turned on his heel and walked back to his stupid car without saying bye.

Noelia quickly turned around herself and shut the door behind her. There was no need to let him think she'd be looking after him driving off.

Who the heck do you think you are? I will have you contacted?

Was he too important to pick up the phone himself? Arrogant was an understatement.

With the door closed safely behind her, she gave in to her frustration and let out a long scream. Feeling only slightly better, she looked down at the business card in her hands.

Rubén Ramírez Armengol, Notary.

Seeing the address of the notary's office, Noelia had to read it twice. And then she read it another time just to make sure she wasn't hallucinating. It didn't make sense. It couldn't be.

Is he really-?

This arrogant ass was the new notary in town?

Chapter Two

Her phone rang two hours later. Even before looking at the display, she knew it was him. No one called her at this time. The notary's office number looked already threatening on her phone.

"Ms. Garrido," a female voice said, "I'm calling from the notary's office."

"Yes?"

"Mr. Ramírez has asked me to let you know that the quote came back at 980€ and that the invoice should be ready in approximately two weeks."

"I'm sorry, did you really just say 980€?" Noelia asked.

"Yes?" The woman on the phone hesitated for a moment. "Would you like me to schedule an appointment with Mr. Ramírez if you have questions regarding the matter?"

The notary's secretary obviously had no idea what this was about.

"No thank you, it's not necessary. Thank you for letting me know."

When Noelia hung up the phone, she had to sit down.

980€??? A dent and some chipped lacquer cost 980€?

She took deep breaths trying to control the sudden feeling of anxiety.

Where should she get that amount of money from? She already had a hard enough time getting to the end of the month with her teacher's salary and the mortgage payments up to her neck. The crazy inflation in the last few years made things tighter than ever before. Olive oil tripled in price just like many other things.

Still, she was happy with her life. The independence from her parents' house was worth a million. She liked her job, loved her little townhouse, going to the beach was free and the sun shone most of the days in Spain. She was happy with what she'd achieved and had no desire for fancy things.

Unforeseen bills, however, were a huge issue when every cent counted at the end of the month. And it was not like she could ask the government for a raise.

Asking her parents wasn't an option either. She knew that things were tight financially for them as well. They'd taken care of her long enough and borrowing money from friends or family was always a bad idea.

No.

Noelia crunched numbers again and again. The problem was that when you already lived extremely frugally, there weren't many opportunities to cut on anymore.

Quitting all unnecessary subscriptions?

Check.

Walk or bike whenever possible?

Check.

Making meal plans and cooking in bulk?

Check.

Drink coffee at home instead of buying a coffee to go?

She didn't even like coffee.

Shopping for cheaper insurance and phone contracts?

Done and done.

If she'd quit chocolate and chips, she could maybe put aside another 15€ a month. She could also cancel her bi-weekly meet-up with her friends for lunch, which would save her another 20€ a month.

No more vices and no more social gatherings with the girls until her debt would be paid off.

She typed 980€ divided by 35€ into her phone's calculator.

Twenty-eight months?

Two years and four months because of a rock? A rock she kicked by accident?

This wasn't fair. And besides, he would never agree to her paying off the invoice in 28 months. Would he?

Noelia opened an email and started typing.

Dear Mr. Ramírez,

Then she deleted it again. This was stupid. He was maybe five, max ten years older than her, not more. She started over again.

Dear Rubén,

Shit, no. This sounded way too personal. After all, he was a notary and an arrogant ass. She wanted to keep things as professional between them as she could with her embarrassing payment proposal.

She deleted the line and started from new.

Dear Mr. Ramírez,

Thank you for informing me about the quote for having the damage to your car fixed. As I currently don't possess such funds, I would like to suggest a payment plan of 35€ a month for the next 28 months.

Kind regards,
Noelia Garrido

She felt so nervous, pressing on send, that it made her nauseous. And then she was angry. Angry about feeling nervous. About caring what Mr. Rubén Ramírez Armengol would think of her.

Would he laugh about the fact that she didn't have that amount of money lying around? He surely didn't look like he had any idea what being tight on money was like.

Rubén Ramírez Armengol didn't let her wait for long. With sweaty hands, Noelia opened the reply to her email.

```
Dear Ms. Garrido,


A 28-month payment plan is absolutely NO
option.
However, I am currently looking for a
cleaning lady to come to my office for two
hours a day, Mondays to Fridays.
If you accept, I'm willing to deduct your
debt at a rate of 10€/hour. This way the
matter will be resolved within 10 weeks.
Otherwise, the payment term of the garage
is net 30 days.
Please let me know ASAP.


Sincerely,
R. Ramírez Armengol
```

Absolutely no option? To let him know ASAP? Noelia couldn't believe her eyes.

Her blood was boiling. Even though she'd already assumed that he wouldn't agree to her suggestion, he could have written his email more politely. Instead, he assumed that she was desperate enough to be his cleaning lady.

Was this guy absolutely insane? What would be next? Serve him coffee?

She decided that R. Ramírez Armengol could ASAP himself in the ass.

Noelia was restless all night.

Whenever she drifted off to a light sleep, Rubén Ramírez stood in front of her, lecturing her about discipline. She woke up, feeling aroused.

No. Not an option! she told herself. No way she would mastur-
bate thinking of him.

And yet, falling asleep again was impossible with the heartbeat pulsing in her swollen pussy.

Noelia spent the early morning hours thinking of options.

Her week was busy enough with teaching, corrections, and
preparing classes for the following day. Finding a part-time job
last minute that paid enough to make 980€ within a month was
impossible. This was Spain after all. Most people her age didn't
make much more than 1000€ a month working full time.

No matter how hard she brainstormed, she couldn't come up
with anything useful. Instead, Noelia had to admit to herself that
the notary's offer wasn't the worst option after all. Ten weeks of
cleaning did sound better than 28 months without chips, chocolate, and lunches with the girls.

Chapter Three

"A uniform? You want me to wear a uniform?"

She couldn't believe her ears.

Mr. Ramírez stood behind his shiny desk holding two folded uniforms in his hands.

"This, Ms. Garrido, is a notary's office. I go to work in a suit and tie. My secretary wears a skirt and blazer and the cleaning lady wears the cleaning lady uniform. I'm *very* strict with appropriate work attire. Now if this is an issue for you, I will gladly have my secretary post the job position on the internet and -."

"No," she interrupted him, feeling panic rising inside of her. "I'll wear the uniform, it's not a problem."

After all, she was here now and she'd decided to pull through with this. Ten weeks of hell and then she'd delete this nightmare from her memory and move on with her happy life.

Before she could change her mind, Noelia signed the work contract, detailing the payment plan to pay off her debt.

———

The uniform looked better than expected. Checking herself out in the bathroom mirror, Noelia had to admit that it suited her quite well.

It was a black button-down dress with short sleeves, white lace cuffs, and a collar. A white apron completed the outfit. The black ballerina shoes she wore were the perfect combination.

María Carmen, the notary's secretary showed her where the cleaning products were stored and gave her a list of the tasks that needed to be done daily as well as some extra tasks that were to be completed during the week. She also instructed her on arming and disarming the alarm and then handed her a key to the office.

María Carmen was friendly but distant. She was probably in her late fifties with gray hair up in a neat bun.

Maybe being dead serious is a requirement to work in the notary's office, Noelia thought.

She started with the washrooms. There was only one for men and one for women. Even though they didn't look dirty at all, she washed the floors, making sure that there was no reason to complain about the quality of her cleaning service.

When Noelia did something, she went all out. If she had agreed to work as a cleaning lady, she'd make sure to be the best cleaning lady in town. So much so that she even removed the old manufacturer sticker below the sink, which had been stuck to it since it left the factory.

Next up on her list were the desks and floors of the offices.

María Carmen had already left while she was cleaning the washrooms but Mr. Ramírez was still in his office. Therefore she decided to start with the reception area, wiping down all counters and the secretary's desk. She then cleaned the big table in the meeting room, making sure it was spotless.

Vacuuming took her a while and then she proceeded to wash the tiled floors. The floors sparkled and it smelled nice and citrusy.

.   .   .

Mr. Ramírez's office was now the only space that she had left on the daily to-do list, but he still hadn't left. She didn't want to start any extra tasks before finishing the mandatory ones so she hesitantly knocked on his office door.

"Come in," he responded.

When he looked at her, his eyes widened. Quickly his arrogant expression returned but his initial reaction was priceless.

He probably thought I'd look like an old lady in the outfit, she thought.

Feeling more confident, she pulled her shoulders back and lifted her chin.

Did he try to humiliate her on purpose? If he did, it certainly backfired on him. Thanks to her feminine hips and small waist, she even made a cleaning lady outfit look sexy. And it seemed that Mr. Stuck Up was just a regular man after all.

Noelia forced a fake smile.

"Are you staying much longer? Your office is the only thing left on my to-do list for today."

"Yes, I will have to stick around longer but go right ahead. Just pretend I'm not here."

Noelia took a deep breath to calm down the anger inside of her bubbling up again.

Pretend he's not there? Is he kidding?

But it's not like she could kick him out of his own office and with only 40 minutes left of her two-hour shift, she had to finish his office rather sooner than later.

Armed with a rag and a spray bottle, she approached his desk. At least he was kind enough to move backward with his office chair, leaving her room to do her job and wipe down his desk. But while this gave her space, she now had him sitting right behind her.

Noelia's heart was racing, as she was wiping down the desk as quickly as possible, feeling his eyes on her. She was 100% sure that he was staring at her ass but she felt too self-conscious to turn around and see if it was true.

Thank goodness the skirt of the uniform went down to her knees, but still. Leaning forward to clean his oversized desk, she felt exposed with the skirt riding up her thighs.

"Thank you," she said, slightly out of breath.

"No. Thank you," he responded.

And it actually felt like he meant it. She almost felt guilty that she now had to vacuum his office and make noise while he was working. But then again, he asked her to come clean at these hours, so it wasn't her fault.

And why the heck was she feeling guilty? If anything, bothering him should give her great satisfaction. It was his fault that she was in this situation right now.

Determined to enjoy making noise and disturb the notary as much as she could, she returned with the vacuum cleaner. She started in the furthest corner from him and forced herself to take her sweet time.

This was easier said than done.

Was it her imagination or could she feel his eyes on her?

Why is it so hot in this office?

Could she open a window or would that be rude? Rude or not, she needed some air. Noelia held her breath when she opened one of the big windows.

Will he complain? she wondered.

But no. He ignored her. He seemed deeply concentrated on some documents.

She continued passing the vacuum cleaner. It was difficult to take her time when all she wanted was to leave the room as quickly as possible. Somehow, she felt like being in his presence erased all her confidence.

Noelia kept her eyes on the floor, making sure to catch every bit of dust. Then she vacuumed behind his desk, enjoying the short moment that his back was to her.

Even his back radiated arrogance. The way he sat there, so straight and full of himself with his stupid perfect suit.

She stared at his neck. It looked so soft yet muscular.

The neck was her favorite body part of a man. The part she held onto when being kissed. And the part she clung to when her body was shaken by an orgasm.

The loud thump of the vacuum cleaner hitting the plant pot made Noelia's heart stop.

Noooooooooo!

Chapter Four

She leaped forward to stop it from falling but the ceramic already shattered into countless pieces across the office floor. The black earth was everywhere.

Shiiiiiiiiit. Why? Why? Why?

This man was nothing but bad luck. Why did bad things keep happening to her when she was close to him?

"I'm so sorry, I will replace the pot. Tomorrow you won't even remember this ever happened."

She didn't dare to look at him.

Noelia kneeled on the floor and quickly picked up some of the broken ceramic pieces. There was so much earth. So much earth!

The notary didn't move, nor did he say anything. He continued with his work as if nothing had happened.

Noelia was mad. Mad at herself for staring at his neck and not paying attention to where she was vacuuming. And mad at him for not offering any help or saying something nice, like telling her not to worry about it. Any reaction would have been better than pretending she didn't exist.

She grabbed a bunch of garbage bags from the cleaning supplies cabinet. One was for the yucca plant and earth until she had a replacement pot. The plant would be fine in it until the next day.

Noelia scooped the black earth together with her bare hands trying to save as much as possible. Spending money to buy new earth wasn't even an option she considered.

The earth was wet, sticking to everything. Probably Mr. Ramírez had watered the plant just that morning. The clean-up would have been faster and easier with a broom but then she would have had to throw out the broom afterwards.

Luckily her uniform was black because she'd look like a mess right now if that weren't the case. The white lace apron had taken a beating and her legs were sprinkled with earth. She probably looked more like a participant in a mud race than the proper cleaning lady they expected at the notary's office.

Would he fire her? After day one? Did the contract say anything about cancellation terms because of broken plant pots and dirtying her uniform?

Nonsense! She pushed away the little voice in her head and concentrated on the task in front of her.

With a big roll of paper towels, she wiped up the remaining earth from the tiled floor. It was incredible how far the earth had flown.

Slowly but surely she worked herself on her hands and knees to Mr. Ramírez's desk. It seemed as if the plant pot's mission was to humiliate her as well because most of the earth had splattered right below his desk.

As hard as Noelia tried, she couldn't stop looking at the notary's fancy brown leather shoes which were dotted with black earth sprinkles all over.

Paper towel after paper towel covered in black dirt landed in the garbage bag and then Mr. Ramírez finally moved backward with his chair to make space for her. She avoided looking up at him and tried cleaning up the mess as quickly as possible.

This was easier said than done, feeling his eyes on her again.

She hated how nervous she felt around him. Every couple of

seconds she pulled on her dress, to make sure it didn't slide up, exposing her too much.

Even though the window let in a nice draft, she knew that her face was red from cleaning up this disaster on her hands and knees.

The area below his desk was clean enough now. She would still have to wash the floors anyhow. Turning around on her knees, keeping her eyes carefully on the floor, she saw the only thing left. A trace of earth sprinkles led right up to the notary's shoes.

Noelia felt her heartbeat in her throat as she cleaned up what must have fallen when he'd moved backward with his chair.

Has he not noticed the dirt on his shoes? she wondered.

Why didn't he try to shake it off at least? She was kneeling right in front of him now, hesitating whether or not she should wipe the dirt off.

Searching for the right answer, she looked up at the notary. Even though she'd felt his eyes on her this whole time, her heart skipped a beat when their eyes finally met.

His eyes were dark and beautiful but most of all, they looked hungry.

She quickly avoided his gaze again, looking back down at his shoes. Obviously, she was imagining all of this. The heat in the office was getting to her.

Fuck it, she thought and wiped off his shoes with a clean paper towel.

It was a delicate task to not smudge the earth into the tiny holes of the shoe laces. Her hands were shaky and her heart was racing. As quickly as she tried to get it over with, it took quite some time.

Done.

Noelia looked back up at the notary who gave her the slightest nod. Maybe he didn't even nod and she was just imagining that he did.

But what she saw next was definitely there, not only in her

imagination. The bulge in his dress pants looked extremely tight and uncomfortable.

Noelia's cheeks were already flushed before but now she turned red like a tomato. Quickly she grabbed the garbage bag and fled the room.

———

In the safety of the small washroom, Noelia splashed cold water on her face, taking deep breaths.

Why was her pussy throbbing? Why did it arouse her what had just happened between them? Did something happen?

Looking into the bathroom mirror, she realized that not only her legs were covered in dirt but she had some in her face and hair as well. If she wasn't careful, she'd have to clean the lady's room again and she was already running late with Mr. Ramírez's office.

Noelia wiped the leftover earth off her chin and forehead and then prepped a bucket of soapy water to wash the floors.

Before leaving the washroom, she took another deep breath.

Don't show him how he affects you Noelia, you're the one in charge here.

Chin up, she returned to his office, avoiding even the slightest look in his direction.

Noelia left the office floors shiny and with a citrusy smell. As quickly as she could she emptied the bucket and tidied up all cleaning supplies. She was already ten minutes past the agreed time of two hours. And she had no desire to be in the notary's office any second longer than necessary.

Do I have to say goodbye? she wondered.

It was rude not to. She had hoped he would leave before her to not have to go back to his office again but it looked like she had no other choice.

Noelia knocked on his door and entered without waiting for a reply.

"I'm done for today. Have a nice evening."

She wished him anything else but a nice evening but she knew that if she needed to come back here for ten weeks, she had to play by the rules.

"See you tomorrow, Ms. Garrido."

He looked up for an instant and then returned to his paperwork.

Better this way, she thought and fled his office.

Chapter Five

Noelia dreaded going back to the notary's office. For some reason, it made her more nervous than a root canal appointment at the dentist.

Distracted all day, she even forgot to give her class homework, and that had *never* happened in her career. Noelia was proud to be known as the teacher who gave homework from the first to the last day of school. She was a strict teacher but the students liked her. They respected her.

Luckily it was Friday already and she'd have the weekend to calm down. Maybe she'd do some yoga and go for a run to distract herself.

Noelia arrived at the notary's office with the Yucca plant inside the terracotta pot from her own terrace. The herbs that used to grow in there before, were now finely chopped up and frozen.

María Carmen had already left but there was a note for Noelia on her desk.

Good afternoon Noelia,
Please clean the windows in Mr. Ramírez's office today.
Thank you, María Carmen

Clean the windows? In his office? With him constantly watching her?

She broke out in a sweat at the mere thought of it. It also meant that today she'd have to be much faster. Quickly she changed into her work uniform in the lady's washroom.

Knowing where things were and which products she had to work with sped up the process. She finished the two washrooms in no time and then proceeded with the secretary's desk, and the meeting room table before emptying the garbage bins.

While vacuuming, her mind wandered. She thought of Rubén Ramírez's dark eyes. The intense gaze when she was kneeling in front of him and their eyes met. She dreaded going into his office again, but she was also excited.

Today she'd put up her hair in a bun and she was wearing her pearl earrings. It looked very sexy with the uniform.

Will he notice? she wondered.

He was arrogant and selfish. He thought he was something better and yet she wanted to look beautiful. She wanted *him* to think that she was beautiful. Beautiful and hot. Because he was hot.

Yes. She'd admitted this to herself. As much as she disliked him, he looked hot.

No. That didn't properly describe him. He was very, *very* hot. Like, don't touch him because you'll burn yourself hot.

Washing the floors was quick, the meeting room and reception area weren't very dirty unless, of course, she'd hit plant pots with the vacuum cleaner.

Checking the time, she was happy to see that she had a full hour left to clean his office and the windows.

With the Yucca plant in her arms, she went to Mr. Ramírez's door. Hugging the terracotta pot gave her a sense of security and the plant was excellent for hiding her face behind it.

"Good afternoon, Ms. Garrido," he greeted.

"Good afternoon, Mr. Ramírez," she answered, avoiding any direct eye contact.

She left the plant in the corner close to his desk and then started vacuuming his office and washing the floors. She moved quickly but concentrated today, not letting the feeling of constantly being watched distract her.

No more accidents, she decided.

The windows were big and high. She needed the small ladder of the supplies closet to be able to reach the top.

Noelia had been convinced that Mr. Ramírez only asked her to clean the windows to mock her and show her who's the boss. But now, getting closer, she realized that the earth explosion yesterday had also splattered across the windows and that a clean up was indeed very necessary.

She tried to think of her weekend while cleaning, to distract herself. But it was impossible.

It took all her concentration to not fall off the ladder while cleaning under the notary's scrutinizing eyes.

Besides needing to keep her balance, she had to make sure that she wasn't revealing her purple underwear under the uniform.

It was a full body workout, cleaning with one hand, holding on to the ladder with the other, while trying to tuck her dress between her knees for modesty.

Was he watching? She couldn't really turn around and look if he did, but she was sure she felt his eyes on her. Or was this just her imagination going wild again?

Something inside of her wanted him to watch her. Wanted

his eyes to look as hungry and wanting as they did yesterday when she had just cleaned off his shoes.

Noelia pushed her silly thoughts away.

He's a pretentious jerk, she reminded herself.

Some months it was like this. She was horny and would jump at almost any man to satisfy her needs. Her brain shut off completely and her pussy took over.

"Have a nice evening Mr. Ramírez."

Noelia was happy with herself. It had taken her exactly two hours to finish everything including the windows and no accidents today. What more could she possibly ask for?

"Ms. Garrido, just a moment."

Noelia's heart skipped a beat. She cleaned the windows, replaced his stupid Yucca plant pot and *now* he was going to fire her?

She pulled her shoulders back and thought of some inappropriate insults.

"Would you be interested in working off your hours faster? I had to move here kind of in a rush and the house I'm renting is in serious need of a deep clean. Ideally, this weekend if you can?"

Noelia needed a second to process his words.

An invitation into the lion's den?

The alarm bells were ringing in her head while her pussy twitched excitedly.

His eyes locked with hers which didn't help her think clearly but she knew she had to hold his gaze.

Her grandfather had explained this to her when she was six years old. If you looked at a dog and he stared back into your eyes, you had to hold his gaze until he'd look away. Otherwise, the dog would think he was the master. With men it was similar and she would not let him intimidate her any longer.

"Will I have to wear the uniform at your house?" she asked.

"The cleaning lady *always* needs to wear the cleaning lady uniform, Ms. Garrido. I really don't get why this is so difficult for you to understand."

"Maybe it's because I'm not a cleaning lady, I am a teacher," she answered.

"Well. I'm not looking for a teacher, I need a cleaning lady."

Noelia felt her blood starting to boil but the prospect of finishing the ten weeks of torture sooner was very tempting.

"Fine!"

"Fine?"

"Yes, fine! I'll do it."

"Great," he said. And then he smiled, making him look even hotter. "Tomorrow morning at 9:00 AM then. You already know where it is, house number 34, right where we first met."

Chapter Six

W aking up with an alarm on the weekend should be illegal. And the fact that the alarm woke her up to clean the house of Rúben Ramírez Armengol made it even worse.

Her life was already screwed up enough the way it was. Why had she agreed to dedicate her weekend to this cleaning job as well? If anything, she was in dire need of a break to process this hell of a week.

Last night she washed the two uniforms and hung them to dry outside before going to bed. She used bleach to get the earth stains out of the white apron. From her bed she watched the uniforms blowing in the wind.

I'm not looking for a teacher, I need a cleaning lady?

Very well then Mr. Ramírez. She'd play along. She'd submit to his stupid game *but* she would make up her own rules.

Yes, he made her nervous each time she saw him, but she knew that he wasn't immune to her presence either. Noelia saw that bulge in his pants and erections didn't lie.

He was attracted to her.

He was attracted to the cleaning lady.

So why not push this a little further and twist things around?

Make *him* uncomfortable. *You want a cleaning lady with a proper uniform, Mr. Ramírez? You'll get one!*

Suddenly Noelia felt excited and full of energy.

Time to shower and get ready for work.

———

When she pressed the doorbell of house number 34, her heart was racing. Noelia felt incredibly nervous.

Leaving the house without underwear was something she'd never done before. It felt exciting and naughty. But now, standing in front of the notary's door, she suddenly wasn't so sure of her idea anymore.

The door opened and -

Jeans!

Rubén Ramírez Armengol was wearing jeans!

The fact that he wasn't dressed in a suit and tie, totally threw her off.

Obviously, he wouldn't spend his weekends at home in a suit and tie. What was she even thinking?

But she wasn't prepared for this. He looked good in a suit but in jeans?

Wow. Just wow!

And he was staring at her.

Why is he staring at me? she wondered.

Oh yes. She'd almost forgotten. Her small uniform adjustments.

She wore her Oxford-style black leather shoes paired with white ruffle ankle socks.

Thanks to some safety pins, the length of the black cleaning lady dress was just a *little bit* shorter now.

Before her adjustments it had ended just below her knees, whereas now the dress ended a hand's width above her knee.

Considering that she went commando, it was dangerously

short. The white lace apron covered up the imperfections of the last-minute uniform improvements.

Noelia restrained her hair into a French braid and wore the white pearl earrings again. Her look was the perfect mix of innocence mixed with naughtiness beyond belief.

Mr. Ramírez opened the door wide and stepped aside to let her in. No greeting, nothing.

Was he speechless?

If so, good. After all, his jeans had made her speechless as well.

There were moving boxes everywhere. The living room had two brown leather sofas, an empty bookshelf, and countless plants.

Noelia frowned, remembering the Yucca plant pot of his office. Hopefully, she didn't need to clean the living room. Otherwise, she'd be busy picking up broken plant pots and earth all day.

"Please start in the bathroom," Mr. Ramírez said, opening a door. "The tiles, the grout, the bathtub, sink and toilet. Everything needs a deep clean."

"No problem. Where are your cleaning products?" she asked.

He opened the bathroom cabinet below the sink. Neatly arranged by size, there was a collection of cleaning products, brushes, sponges, and anything else you could possibly desire for a spring clean.

"That should do," she said.

She expected him to leave but he just stood there, waiting.

Was he expecting her to say anything else?

Noelia bent down to look into the cabinet and examined the collection of cleaning supplies. She forgot to bend her knees on purpose, assuring him a good view below her skirt. Maybe not enough to see that she wasn't wearing any underwear but definitely a generous amount of her thighs.

She felt his eyes on her but she wanted to make sure that this time, she wasn't only imagining things. When she turned her head to check, his eyes met hers. She forgot to breathe as the electric jolt traveled through her body. Her pussy twitched.

"Are the products to your satisfaction, Ms. Garrido?"

"Yes. I appreciate good quality products. I will get to work right away and take care of all the *dirty* things around here Mr. Ramírez."

Noelia couldn't help but smile. She started to like this game. Especially now, that she was the one making up the rules.

She waited, holding his gaze until he turned to leave.

Ha! she silently cheered.

She won this round.

Time to clean!

The bathroom was tiled all the way up to the ceiling and the grout was discolored almost everywhere. This project would take her a while.

In order to reach the top row of the tiles, Noelia climbed up on the bathtub rim. Then she sprayed and scrubbed and sprayed and scrubbed. She was happy to see that the cleaning product worked quite well removing the build-up of dirt and grime.

"What are you doing?"

Mr. Ramírez's voice startled her.

Noelia had been so absorbed in her meditative task that she didn't even hear him approach behind her. Quickly she held on to the wall to not lose balance. Her Oxford-style shoes weren't exactly great for balancing on the tub.

She took a deep breath to collect herself before turning towards him, putting on a smile.

Oh yes, she realized. From down there he could definitely see under her skirt.

"I'm dealing with some dirty business, Mr. Ramírez?"

"Nonsense! You're putting yourself in danger! Get down right now, I will get the step ladder!"

Noelia jumped off the bathtub rim and waited.

Mr. Ramírez returned shortly after with a small 3-step ladder.

"Here," he said. "Try this."

He held on to the step ladder as she climbed up the three steps. It was almost sweet that he made sure she was safe.

Rubén Ramírez was so close to her. So close to her naked pussy. What if he'd just slide up the skirt and start licking her? His face was right there already. At the perfect height.

Shall I lift my dress and press his face between my legs? she wondered.

No.

She couldn't.

He was the notary and she had a work contract with him. What if he sued her for sexual harassment? She'd never stand a chance.

Noelia started scrubbing the tiles again, waiting for him to let go of the step ladder but he didn't.

After about a minute of scrubbing, she stopped and looked down at him and that's when she saw it.

His eyes. That look. The hunger. The lust in them.

Yes!

Her plan was working.

"Thank you Mr. Ramírez, I'm perfectly safe now, you can let go."

He let go of the step ladder and turned to leave. When he was already halfway out of the bathroom he stopped and turned around.

"Once you're done here, please come see me in the living room, Ms. Garrido. We have to address the issue you seem to have with proper work attire."

Chapter Seven

"I'm done with the bathroom."

The notary looked up. He was busy putting books from a box onto the bookshelf.

"Wait here," he answered and left her standing alone in the room.

A short moment later he returned.

"Good. You did a great job with the bathroom, Ms. Garrido. What I'm not happy with though, is how you are wearing your uniform today."

Noelia looked down at herself.

"You don't like my shoes, Mr. Ramírez?"

She tried her best not to burst out laughing.

"The shoes are not the problem."

"Is it my French braid? Do you prefer my hair up in a bun like yesterday?"

Mr. Ramírez stepped towards her and then slowly walked around her until he stopped right behind her. His hand wrapped around her braid and pulled on it, tilting her chin up.

The unexpected touch, gentle yet firm, made her legs feel weak. He was so close to her. Nothing touched her besides his hand holding on to her braid. And yet, she felt his heat radiate. Felt his breath on her ear.

"No. The braid isn't the problem either," he said and let go of her hair.

Noelia didn't dare to move or say anything. Her pussy was pulsating excitedly.

"Take the apron off," he commanded.

She opened the bow of the white apron and took it off as told.

Then he examined the uniform, his fingers carefully inspecting the countless safety pins she'd used to shorten the dress.

Even though his hands touched the fabric only, her skin felt burning hot wherever his fingertips passed by.

"I see," he said, still standing behind her. "Now bend forward and touch your toes, Ms. Garrido."

Is he serious?

She knew it was her own fault, leaving the house without underwear. She'd wanted him to see it. A peak of it. A peak to leave him wondering if she wore panties or not.

But this?

He stood right behind her. He wouldn't just get a peak, he'd get the widescreen HD version of her pussy!

The thought of him looking at her like that aroused her. She imagined that hungry look in his eyes.

"I said, bend forward and touch your toes!"

His voice was strict, leaving no room for discussion.

Noelia closed her eyes and then slowly bent forward. Thanks to her regular Yoga workouts she was flexible enough to put her palms on the floor comfortably.

She took shallow breaths, feeling the cool draft on her moist pussy. There was no doubt on her mind anymore whether or not the skirt was short enough to fully expose her.

Mr. Ramírez circled once completely around her and then stopped behind her again.

Noelia didn't dare to move. She felt her face turning red from the blood flowing down to her head.

"I believe that the first time you came to my office, I informed you that I'm *very* strict with appropriate work attire. Have I or have I not?"

"Yes, you have, Mr. Ramírez."

"And yet, you have decided to do the opposite and provoke me."

Noelia waited for him to continue his lecture. Her position was getting uncomfortable but knowing that he was looking at her pussy made it totally worth it.

"I believe, Ms. Garrido, what you need is some discipline. Wouldn't you agree?"

Noelia wondered if he could see her pussy dripping right now.

"Yes, Mr. Ramírez."

"And do you remember what my definition of discipline is?"

"Yes, Mr. Ramírez."

"What is the definition of discipline, Ms. Garrido?"

"Discipline is if you would take me over your knee and give me a spanking."

The blood rushed through her pussy. This was the hottest and at the same time strangest situation she'd ever been in.

"Good," he said. "I'm glad you remember. I will sit down now and let you reflect on this a little bit. If you agree that some discipline is in order you will come and get over my knee. Otherwise, please take your things and go home and I'll see you on Monday in the office in a more appropriate uniform."

Chapter Eight

Noelia didn't move.

She knew what she wanted. She'd wanted it from the day she met him and he mentioned spanking for the first time.

But fantasizing about it and actually ending up in that particular situation, were two completely different pairs of shoes.

Will he stop if I ask him to? What if she couldn't handle the spanking?

Two minutes passed before Noelia gathered the courage, lifted up from her uncomfortable position, and walked over to Mr. Ramírez.

She avoided direct eye contact, feeling too shy to look at him after she'd just flashed all her private parts to him. He gave her an approving little nod.

"Take off your dress. I don't want you to get poked by all those needles."

Noelia instantly regretted shortening the dress with all those safety pins. The longer dress would have covered her, protected her, and saved her from having to strip down naked in front of the notary.

But without the adjustment of her uniform, she wouldn't be in this situation right now. This crazy hot situation.

Noelia blushed already at the thought of taking her dress off but then she did it anyway. She had made her decision and she wouldn't back out now. Her craving to get spanked by Mr. Ramírez was way too strong. She knew that if she chickened out now and missed out on this opportunity, she would regret it forever.

With nothing but her folded arms covering her breasts, she stood next to the notary. Noelia felt her heartbeat in her swollen pussy as she looked down at her feet. She knew he was watching her.

Then his hand wrapped around her wrist. His grip was firm but gentle at the same time. Slowly he guided her over his knees.

The feeling of the rough jeans fabric on her soft skin was a reminder of the drastic contrast. He was fully dressed and she was completely naked, only wearing the white ruffle ankle socks and her black shoes.

Mr. Ramírez adjusted her position so that she touched the floor with her hands. This way her bottom was centered on his lap, exposing everything right there in front of his eyes. Noelia didn't think she could blush even more but the heat in her face confirmed otherwise.

How can this be so embarrassing but feel so thrilling at the same time? she wondered.

He put his hand on her bottom. It felt warm and calming.

"Ready?" he asked.

"Yes," she answered automatically but wondered how she could ever be ready for this.

When he lifted his hand, Noelia held her breath.

This is it, she thought.

SMACK.

Her bottom shook. His hand was still on her cheek. The slap had been firm but not too harsh.

It felt good.

It stung a bit but with his hand on her skin now, it just felt good. Good and very arousing.

SMACK.

Noelia's left cheek got the same attention as her right one.

Two slaps only and she could feel herself dripping already. And if she could feel the drip, then Mr. Ramírez could surely see it.

Is he looking at my needy cunt right now with that hungry look in his eyes?

If only he would touch her. *There.*

SMACK.

His hand landed on the other cheek again in the same spot as before. It was only an instant this time, that he let her process the intense sensation before moving on to the other side again.

SMACK.

Noelia indulged in the vibrations that radiated straight to her pussy.

Less nervous now, she tried to get more comfortable, adjusting her hands on the floor.

Another slap shook her bottom. Again, Mr. Ramírez had aimed for the same spot and the stingy pain started to get uncomfortable.

His hands were large. She had noticed that when he signed her job contract. Now she realized what this meant for her backside. His palms were almost like a paddle and covered not only the lower part of her bottom but also a part of her upper thigh.

After giving the other side three hard smacks in a row, he rubbed both her cheeks.

Wow!

Would he play with her pussy now? Did he notice her body telling him that she needed that?

She spread her legs a tiny bit, to encourage him. To let him know that he had her approval to touch her wherever he wanted.

"Ms. Garrido! You've ended up in exactly this position for repeatedly provoking me with your inappropriate outfit and behavior. Do you really think spreading your legs now will get you out of this situation any faster?"

"No Sir."

No Sir?

Where did that come from?

It had just slipped out. Her brain had shut off and her needy pussy had taken over again. He drove her crazy.

"I will start with your spanking now, Ms. Garrido, prepare yourself."

Start? Prepare yourself?

She thought he was done. What was he talking about?

His hand tightened around her waist, locking her in. And then it started. He started.

Smack after smack rained down on her butt. The noise of skin hitting skin echoed in Mr. Ramírez's empty living room. In no time Noelia's grunts and moans mixed with the slapping sounds.

One second she clenched her teeth together, deciding to not give him any reaction, and the next second she was huffing and puffing with her legs lifting and kicking.

He stopped, but only to lock her legs in with his own.

Now she really couldn't move anymore. The short pause as well as the feeling of being completely at his mercy now made her pussy gush.

Fantasizing about him spanking her was great but this?

"Ms. Garrido, if you ever need me to stop, please tell me. But we both know that you need and you deserve a hard spanking."

Can this man be any hotter? she wondered, indulging in the throbbing feeling between her legs.

"Can we continue?" he asked.

Noelia had to swallow to find her voice. Her throat was dry from the moaning and heavy breathing.

"Yes Mr. Ramírez," she answered.

Her "yes" was all he needed.

His hand came down hard. She wasn't sure if he'd increased his intensity even more or if it felt like that because her backside was so sore already from before. If she weren't safely locked in by his leg across the back of her knees, she'd be surely falling off his lap from kicking now.

The burning sensation.

The sharp sting of each whack.

Her butt was on fire.

SMACK! SMACK! SMACK! SMACK!

No break, no gentle touch. She was getting spanked.

Hard.

Her body was fighting it, her back arching but Mr. Ramírez's elbow pressed her back down in place without stopping to dish out his no-nonsense discipline.

Noelia gave up on trying to not make noise. She let go completely, squeaking, grunting, and crying out with every slap.

When he stopped she was relieved but missed his touch at the same time. As if he knew, he put his hand back on her cheeks. His hand was just lying there, not moving for a moment and then he started to rub her butt gently.

Noelia was completely out of breath. Her heart was still racing.

Mr. Ramírez took his leg off her and also loosened his grip around her waist.

"Put your upper body on the sofa," he said and shifted slightly so that she could do what he said. The cold leather touched her flushed face. It smelled and felt good.

She was comfortable now, feeling completely relaxed. His hand kept on rubbing her butt for a while.

He didn't say anything and neither did Noelia. She indulged in this intimate moment, wanting it to last forever.

It felt so good.

She still craved his touch somewhere else but she didn't dare to spread her legs again. To provoke him, again.

The spanking was hard. It was hot. It was what she'd always

wanted to experience but another one? Her butt could not possibly handle any more today.

"Now get up and take those safety pins out of your uniform. Once you're dressed appropriately, you can start on the kitchen cabinets."

Chapter Nine

Two weeks passed by without any incidents. Ever since that eventful Saturday, Noelia walked around with a permanent smile on her face. Apart from that, her pussy had not stopped being swollen.

It was as if all the blood had collected down there when she got spanked by Mr. Ramírez and now it was stuck there, constantly stimulating her.

He'd gotten friendlier after the spanking and even told her that she could call him Rubén when they were at his house. In the office, however, he insisted on being addressed by his last name.

Teaching mathematics and physics to teenagers in her constant state of arousal was extremely difficult. The time dragged on in the classroom each day and she couldn't wait for 5:00 PM to come around to go to her other job.

To go see *him* again.

She had a good cleaning routine now at the notary's office. When she started working for Mr. Ramírez, she did his office last because she dreaded going there. Whereas now, she did it last because she wanted to save the best for last.

Feeling his eyes on her while she cleaned his office had

become her drug. A kinky addiction. Sometimes their eyes met for a second, causing that crazy rush of adrenaline in her body.

It was difficult to not stare at his big hands when he worked at his desk. She constantly wondered if he'd spank her again. If he thought of it as much as she did.

Noelia knew she couldn't show up with an inappropriate outfit at the notary's office but she did play with different ideas that would possibly get her his attention.

As more and more time passed, she wondered if everything had just been a very realistic dream. Had she imagined everything? Maybe she was mentally ill, mixing up fantasy and reality.

"Ms. Garrido, can I speak to you in my office please?"

Noelia had just arrived at work and switched into her uniform when the notary's dark voice startled her. She'd never seen him out of his office.

"Of course Mr. Ramírez," she answered.

She felt her heart accelerating when she followed behind him to his office. Even though she preferred him in jeans, his ass did look gorgeous in those dress pants.

Rubén walked into the office first and then held the door open for her. He gave her a strange look.

Noelia got even more nervous.

What's going on? she wondered.

The sound of the door shutting gave her goosebumps. Theoretically, there was no need to close the door, they were the only ones in the office now.

Noelia knew she was in trouble. It scared and excited her at the same time. She was scared because she didn't want to lose her job. Her only chance of seeing him every day. And excited because she *wanted* something to happen. She'd been waiting for it. Hoping for it every day she came to her cleaning job.

Mr. Ramírez had his back to the door.

"Ms. Garrido, did you do it on purpose or not?"

Did what on purpose? What was he talking about?

Searching for a clue, she looked at him.

"I see," he said before she could even reply.

"You forgot to empty my garbage bin yesterday. When clients come to my office, I need this space to be spotless and tidy. I do not want them to see which chocolate brand I prefer."

Noelia tried to hide her smile. She knew exactly which chocolate was his favorite. She also knew that he emptied a pack of salty pistachios every other day and that he drank his coffee black. A garbage bin did spill lots of secrets.

"I'm very sorry Mr. Ramírez, it won't happen again."

He didn't seem to be happy with her apology. He waited, his intense eyes watching her.

Do it! Spank me! she thought.

She wanted it. She wanted it so badly. What was he waiting for? For her to ask him? But what if not?

No matter what, she couldn't. Asking for it would be way too embarrassing.

"Do you think you'll learn your lesson with *just* an apology Ms. Garrido?"

She blushed.

It was clear what he insinuated. Noelia looked at the floor, gathering the courage to answer.

"I'm not sure, Mr. Ramírez. I think-. I might need some discipline to remember my tasks better next time."

Her pussy throbbed. Noelia couldn't believe what she'd just said out loud. What she'd literally just asked him to do.

Mr. Ramírez didn't say anything. The moment of silence between them seemed endless.

Finally, Noelia lifted her gaze, not able to handle the tension any longer. She looked right into Rubén's eyes. And they were hungry.

"Put your hands against the wall," he said, pointing behind her.

Noelia was surprised but she did as told. She walked over to the spot he'd pointed at. The wall felt coolish on the palms of her hands. It was a soothing feeling.

The sound of his dress shoes on the tiled floors gave away that he was approaching behind her.

He didn't hesitate a second. The notary lifted her dress and then pulled her thong down to her ankles.

Instantly, the goosebumps were back. It felt weird to stand fully exposed in his office. That mixture of feeling vulnerable but also incredibly aroused. It felt so right yet so wrong.

Mr. Ramírez was next to her now and wrapped his arm around her belly holding on to her waist. His smell surrounded her, distracting her for a second. He was so close to her. Closer than ever before. His grip was like a tight hug and it was the best feeling ever.

SMACK! SMACK! SMACK! SMACK!

Mr. Ramírez's hand came down quickly and persistently. The impact was just hard enough to cause a bit of a sting and make her butt jiggle nonstop.

Noelia indulged in the feeling of his body pressing against hers while he was spanking her. Despite the rough treatment of her backside, she felt safe and protected in his arms.

At this speed his hand will be tired soon, she thought.

But Rubén had no trouble continuing for a much longer time. He made sure Noelia's butt resembled the red of the thong she wore under her uniform.

When he finally stopped, her cheeks were sizzling. She could feel the heat radiating from her skin.

The grip around her waist loosened up and then he let go of her. Noelia immediately ached for his closeness.

"Go bend over my desk," he said in a very calm voice.

Chapter Ten

B *end over his desk? Oh yes, please fuck me! Please!*
  Excited, Noelia shuffled over to his desk in small steps.
She didn't dare to pull up or take off her underwear, so they still
dangled at her ankles, restricting her movement.

When she arrived at his desk she turned around to look at
Rubén, who gave her a reassuring nod. She made sure to lift her
dress, before bending over the notary's desk. The shiny wood felt
coolish on her forearms and face.

How long had she been waiting for this? She wanted him so
badly. To feel him inside of her.

He walked to the other side of the desk and opened a
drawer.

Is he fetching the condoms? she wondered.

She closed her eyes, waiting impatiently for his return.
Luckily, he didn't make her wait for long. Suddenly he was
right behind her, the soft fabric of his dress pants touching her
skin.

"Spread your cheeks for me, Ms. Garrido." His voice was
hoarse.

Wow! He really is a kinky one, she thought.

Noelia's pussy throbbed intensely as she did as told, showing

44

him *everything*. She was more than ready for his cock. He would slip right in.

The liquid dripping on her spread cheeks surprised Noelia.

Lube? Didn't he see that she was soaking wet? There was no need for lube.

Suddenly something cold and hard pushed against her tight butthole. Noelia let go of her spread cheeks and squirmed sideways.

"Spread your cheeks and don't move. I won't hurt you, it's just a small plug," he said.

His voice was very calm but decisive.

Did he just say plug?

The confidence of the notary had driven her crazy from the day she'd met him. But as much as it bothered her, it made her feel safe. She didn't like to admit it but she wanted him to take charge. All she had to do was let go and follow his instructions.

She was scared of having something inserted into her virgin butt. But more than scared, she was curious and very very aroused. The fact that it was so wrong and so dirty, made it even more exciting. And if butt plugs turned Rubén on, then she wanted to try it. She wanted to try everything with him. Please him, like no other woman had ever pleased him before.

Noelia tried to relax on the desk, then decisively grabbed her warm cheeks and spread them apart. She took a deep breath as the cold metal toy slid up and down her lubed bottom and then searched her tight entrance again. Rubén rubbed and pushed the steel plug against her.

When the tip of the steel plug settled into the nook of her tight booty hole, Noelia's buttocks suddenly opened up, sucking in the plug.

She gasped for air. There was an instant of discomfort when the thickest part of the plug stretched her out, but before she could complain, the plug had already settled inside of her.

It was in.

And it felt good. Good, strange, and oh so naughty at the same time.

Mr. Ramírez let her adjust to the new sensations for a short moment. Then he tugged lightly on the plug which brought on another wave of arousal spreading through her body.

"This plug is now part of your uniform, I'm expecting you to wear it when you come to work. Let it be a reminder to not forget any of your tasks. You can go back to work now Ms. Garrido."

What?

That was all? Did he really leave her hanging with a dripping wet pussy? Why wasn't he fucking her? She needed to get fucked right now!

Should she say it? Beg for it? Is that what he wanted?

"Ms. Garrido, I said you can get back to work now. I don't have all day."

Noelia blushed. She felt embarrassed but more than anything she was angry.

Who does he think he is? she wondered.

She pushed herself up from his desk and then stalled, feeling the plug twisting inside of her. For an instant, she was distracted but the last thing she wanted was another reminder of Mr. Ramírez to get out. Quickly, she pulled up her underwear and fled the office, avoiding any eye contact with him.

Concentrating on cleaning was almost impossible. The plug was quite heavy, twisting and turning inside of her every time she moved. And when she cleaned, she moved nonstop.

He didn't have all day? Pah! Then why did he call her into his office to begin with?

She was late with all her tasks now because of him. And she

was the one with a plug in her ass. It was also she who had been left with a dripping wet and needy pussy.

So what exactly was *his* problem?

Noelia scrubbed the insides of the men's toilet aggressively with the toilet brush. She hurried to catch up for the lost time but she kept on getting distracted. With every step she took, the plug shifted and aroused her so much that her pussy just wouldn't stop throbbing.

Determined to finish her tasks on time, she continued to clean the sink. Then she stretched up to her tippy toes to reach all edges of the big mirror on top of the sink.

Fuck, this plug feels incredible.

She wanted to see what it looked like.

Just a quick little peak, she thought.

Chapter Eleven

Noelia locked the door just in case. Then she turned away from the mirror, pulled down her underwear, and lifted her uniform. She twisted her head to look at herself in the mirror.

Her bottom was still a bit red and right there between her rosy cheeks she could see it. Just like before, she spread her butt cheeks and approached the mirror to get a closer look. Only once she touched the end of the steel plug, she realized that it was a little loop. Her finger fit right into it. She twisted and tugged on it while watching herself in the mirror.

Overwhelmed by the arousal rushing through her body, Noelia quickly pulled her thong back up. Her face was flushed when she faced the mirror again.

She splashed a handful of cold water into her face to calm down but leaning against the sink had the opposite effect on her. The edge of the sink pushed right against her swollen pussy and she unconsciously rubbed herself on it for a moment.

It'll just be a minute, she told herself.

She'd quickly bring herself to orgasm to calm down her pussy and then she'd be able to concentrate on work again. The bathroom was already locked anyway and there was no way she could continue working like this.

Her right hand slid down between her legs while she held onto the sink with her left. Noelia closed her eyes and thought of being bent over Mr. Ramírez desk again, just that in her fantasy he did indeed fuck her. He fucked her hard.

Rubbing the thin moist fabric of her underwear back and forth on her clit was just the right amount of stimulation.

The rubbing, the sensations of the butt plug, and her fantasy of getting a rough pounding tipped her over the edge within moments. She leaned on the sink for support as her knees buckled from the sheer power of the pulsations in her pussy. The orgasm radiated deep into her ass, as her booty hole contracted tightly around the plug.

Just a little bit more. One more orgasm and then I can concentrate again, she thought, and continued rubbing herself.

The knocking ripped her out of her fantasy. Noelia watched the door handle move. Someone was trying to come in. Then there was more knocking.

"Ms. Garrido, open the door!"

Fuck!

Noelia quickly pushed herself up from the sink and then unlocked the door. She put a smile on her face and then opened the door wide, trying to act normal.

"Mr. Ramírez, are you leaving already?"

"What were you doing in there?" he asked, completely ignoring her question.

Noelia blushed.

He knew. He knew exactly what she'd been up to in there.

"I was cleaning, Mr. Ramírez," she answered.

His eyes locked with hers and even though she had just felt hot and sweaty, she now broke out in chills. She tried holding his intense gaze but her eyelashes fluttered and she couldn't avoid blinking.

"I don't like it when people lie to me, Ms. Garrido. So let's try again, what were you doing in there?"

Noelia didn't know what to say. She wouldn't admit to what she did. It was his fault after all. He did this to her, leaving her hanging like he did. Leaving her dripping and unsatisfied after playing with her.

"Show me your hands," he demanded.

"What? Why?"

"Show me your hands," he repeated, his voice strict.

Reluctantly, Noelia lifted her hands.

Did he have some fortunetelling skills, reading her hands to find out what she did?

But Mr. Ramírez didn't look at her hands. Instead, he took both her hands in his and lifted them to his-

Oh no! Noelia thought. She tried to pull them away but his grip was firm.

Rubén put her hands against his face and inhaled deeply without stopping to stare right into her eyes.

A slight smirk appeared on his face and Noelia blushed even darker red.

"I see," he said.

He gently put her hands down before letting go of them.

Will he fire me now? she wondered. She held her breath.

"Yes, I'm leaving. Please lock up and activate the alarm system before you go. Have a nice evening!"

Chapter Twelve

Noelia wore the anal plug to work every day. It did make cleaning a lot more interesting. This plug brought being aroused to a whole new level.

She was on high alert every second at the notary's office. Even though she had a hard time not touching herself, she never gave in to her cravings again.

No more masturbating. No more masturbating at the notary's office.

She hadn't seen Mr. Ramírez since Monday, the day he caught her. Every time she opened the door to his office and he wasn't there, her heart sank. It was Friday now and she didn't even know if he was expecting her to help him at his house again this weekend.

Cleaning the office when he wasn't around was kind of boring. The only thing she enjoyed was cleaning his office. It smelled like him and she felt close to him when she was in there.

Mr. Ramírez didn't need to worry about her forgetting the garbage bin when he wasn't there. It was the only information she could get about him, she'd never miss out on that.

Today he ate an apple, a banana, and a bag of cashew nuts.

Cashews? Did they run out of pistachios at the supermarket? And no chocolate. Weird.

Madre mía, Noelia, you're a freaking stalker, she thought.

This was crazy. She was crazy. No! *He drove* her crazy!

One rock. One tiny rock. And now her life was upside down.

Here she was, a respectable math and physics teacher, in a cleaning lady uniform and a butt plug up her ass, looking through the garbage bin of the arrogant guy who did this to her.

And why? Because she missed him. Because she wanted to know how his day was. She wanted to know if he was okay and why he skipped the chocolate. She cared about him even though she didn't want to.

It made her angry and sad and a little bit more crazy. And the butt plug drove her crazy too.

Oh my god! The fucking butt plug. It was so so *so* good. Maybe that was the problem? Maybe it pressed on some blood vessel that was directly connected to her brain, blocking her from thinking clearly.

Wiping his desk, she spotted it. An envelope with *Ms. Noelia Garrido* written in cursive handwriting on it. Her heart stopped.

He left a note!

He left me a note! For me! From him!

She ripped it open immediately. Patience was definitely not her forté.

His handwriting was neat, tiny, and cursive.

Dear Noelia,

I'm sorry I couldn't ask you in person but I'd be very happy if you would help me again this weekend at my house. Around 9 a.m.?

I understand if you have other plans.

Rubén

Noelia's heart was racing. She read the letter again. And again.

Even though she was in the office he wrote *Noelia* and not Ms. Garrido. This letter was friendly and personal. This letter was not from Mr. Ramírez, it was from Rubén. And it would make him *very happy* if she could come.

She clutched the letter to her chest. In 15 hours she would finally see him again.

———

Rubén opened the door with a big smile on his face. He was either having a very good day or he was truly happy to see her. Noelia hoped for the latter.

"Come, there is lots of work waiting for us," he said.

He looked gorgeous. Blue washed-out jeans and a white T-shirt. Rubén let her pass in front of him which was a real shame because she loved staring at his neck, his wide shoulders, and that juicy ass. Now, instead of looking at him, she could feel his eyes on her. Instinctively she pulled her shoulders back and lifted her chin. She didn't feel confident but she knew how to pretend that she did.

"Keep on walking, we're working on the backyard this weekend."

Stepping outside, Noelia needed a moment to take everything in.

Wow.

There was lots of wood piled up in a corner. A sawhorse was set up and on the floor was an open toolbox. Lots of huge bags of earth were leaning against the fence.

"Over there will be the vegetable patch and here I want to put a raised garden bed," Rubén explained. "Can you start on taking out the weeds?"

He held out purple gardening gloves. Women-sized gardening gloves.

Did he buy them for me? Noelia wondered. They did look brand new.

"Sure," she answered, snatching the gloves.

This sounded so much better than cleaning the grout in between the hundreds of floor tiles.

Noelia was convinced that no one had ever enjoyed removing weeds this much. As she ripped out grasses and roots, she watched Rubén taking out the saw and cutting piece after piece for the garden beds and stands. The spring sun was hot and there was no shade in the backyard. Shortly after he started working, Rubén took off his T-shirt.

Plucking weeds while watching a topless eye candy doing some wood-working. Can life be any better?

She wasn't surprised to see a six-pack on him. His arms and shoulder muscles tensed up while he sawed, drilled, and hammered away.

Whenever Rubén turned around, she quickly looked down. This game went on for hours until all the weeds were out and several garden shelves and beds were assembled.

"You're dirty Noelia."

She grinned. Was the double meaning intentional?

"I know, but you look like breaded chicken."

She passed a finger along his shoulder and then held it up to show him the layer of sawdust.

Rubén smiled at her, his eyes sparkling. Noelia held her breath, smiling back at him.

For a moment the world stood still.

If this was a Hollywood movie, he'd kiss me now, she thought.

"It's definitely time for a shower. Shall we continue at the same time tomorrow?" he asked.

Or I could join you in the shower, she thought.

She tried her best to hide her disappointment. This wasn't a Hollywood movie.

"Sure," she answered.

"Oh, and one more thing," he said.

Her heart skipped a beat.

"Yes?"

"You can come in your regular clothes tomorrow but the plug is still obligatory."

Chapter Thirteen

As much as she'd been complaining about her uniform, Noelia now wished she could wear it.

First, she put on a pair of jeans but she wasn't sure if the butt plug was showing so she switched to a skirt. The skirt made her feel overdressed in case they'd be gardening again so she went back to jeans.

In the end, she combined the dark blue high-rise jeans with a tucked-in red t-shirt and red ballerinas. Turning and twisting in front of the big mirror in her entrance, she checked to see if the butt plug was showing. She was sure that it did but you would only notice if you knew about it. And Rubén knew anyway.

"Let's go," Rubén said, closing the door behind him.

Noelia followed him to his car. The dent was fixed. There was no trace of the damage anymore. The car garage had done a great job.

She was surprised when Rubén held the passenger door open for her and then closed it once she was sitting down and buckled in. The last time someone opened and closed a car door for her was when she was a child.

Rubén got into the car and started the motor. He looked over to Noelia and their eyes met for a second before he drove off.

He looks excited, she thought.

Being in such a small enclosed space with him was nerve-wracking. The radio played some song, but she didn't even hear it. She put her hands on her legs, secretly wiping the sweat off on her jeans.

"Where are we going?" she finally asked.

"To the garden center."

Shopping with him was a lot of fun. He asked her for her opinion and let her pick out things. Rubén seemed happy like a kid in a candy store. He took his time to look at every single plant.

"I've never seen anyone so excited about picking out which tomato variety to plant," she teased him.

His eyes changed from sparkling to soft.

"I love it. As a kid, I spent a lot of time in my grandparents' garden. I had my own little tools and they showed me how to take care of the plants. I miss them a lot but when I work in the garden, I feel like they're still with me. Does that make sense?"

Noelia felt a knot in her throat, so she just nodded, imagining a tiny version of Rubén gardening with his grandparents.

He'd caught her off guard. She wasn't prepared for this. She wasn't prepared to actually like him.

Almost two hours later they arrived back at the house with the trunk full of seedlings, buckets, and plants. The back seats were folded down to make space for all the things Rubén had bought.

Noelia had a small lemon tree between her legs. She couldn't move and had to wait for Rubén to open the door and free her.

When he bent down to pick up the tree, he was so close that she could smell him. Noelia took a deep breath of Rubén.

So good. So, so good.

Calm the fuck down, Noelia! You're his cleaning lady, nothing else, she reminded herself.

But she was also a cleaning lady that had a stainless steel plug up her butt which turned her on nonstop. Since the day he pushed the plug inside of her, she'd been waiting for him to double-check if she was actually wearing it as instructed.

Did he forget about it?

When she came over the first time and provoked him in her too-short uniform, she didn't care about him. It was a game, nothing else.

But now, things were different. Things were complicated. Because she did care. And not just a bit. She cared a lot about him.

This side of Rubén drove her crazy. The hot guy in jeans who loved gardening, because it reminded him of his grandparents, was so different from the arrogant man in a suit who gave her shit when she accidentally hit his car with the rock. He was different from the uptight notary in the office. And yet, he was the same person.

"I wish I could read your mind right now," Rubén interrupted Noelia's thoughts.

She immediately blushed.

Rubén laughed.

"Now I *really* want to know what you were thinking. I bet it was something dirty," he said.

"No!" she defended herself but turned even redder.

Fuck! Why do I always have to blush?

She hated this about herself. She wished she could stop it but around Rubén it was even worse.

"Do you know how much it excites me when you blush, Noelia?"

She ignored his comment. Her mouth was dry and she

turned away from Rubén, pretending she was busy taking out the plants.

His hand grabbed her arm firmly, turning her around to face him.

"Tell me! What were you thinking about?"

His voice was soft and he was smiling, his eyes sparkling.

Noelia was a horrible liar, there was no purpose in even trying.

"I thought of how different you are here compared to when I damaged your car or when you are at work."

"You think I'm different when I'm at home?" he asked.

"Yes."

"Different from the man telling you that discipline means taking you over my knee and giving you a spanking?"

Noelia stared into Rubén's eyes. Did he expect an answer? There was a mischievous grin on his face.

"Different from the man who spanked you in the office and then pushed a plug into your beautiful round ass?"

She turned her head as she felt the heat rise in her face again.

Rubén's hand touched her cheek, gently pushing, to make her look at him again.

"It's all me, Noelia. I might wear jeans instead of a suit and obviously, I'm more relaxed in my house than at work where I have to act professionally. But my mind Noelia-. My mind is always dirty. No matter where I am, I imagine spanking you and doing dirty things to you. And making you ask for it. That's me."

All the blood from her head rushed down to Noelia's pussy. Her butt contracted tightly around the plug and her knees felt so weak suddenly, she thought she might faint.

His hand which was wrapped around her arm was the only support.

Will he catch me if I faint?

"Come on, let's get the things to the backyard," he said.

Chapter Fourteen

Noelia and Miguel snatched their favorite corner table on the bar's terrace. It was a busy area in town with lots of pedestrians passing by, but the table had a bit more distance from the other guests, giving them some privacy to talk.

"Oh my god, you're living my dream! That's the hottest thing ever!" Miguel said.

She laughed. It felt so good to finally tell someone and Miguel was her best friend. Her *gay* best friend. He kept all her secrets and gave the best advice.

"Yeah, I figured that I'd have your full attention mentioning the butt plug," she teased.

"Well, it's not just any kind of plug. It's a stainless steel plug! I'm telling you, Noelia, this man has class. He's a total keeper!"

Noelia sighed and took a sip of her *Tinto De Verano*.

"But that's the problem," she said. "I can't keep what I don't have. Nothing has happened since and I just feel like he's playing his stupid game with me. Meanwhile, I see this sensitive and sweet side of him and you know -. I like him. I really *really* like him. I want more. I need more. I go crazy in his presence not being able to touch him or kiss him-." Noelia smiled, thinking of

Rubén. "Don't get me wrong, I love getting spanked but more than anything I want a hug from him. Am I weird?"

Miguel took Noelia's hands in his.

"No, not weird at all. It's called falling in love," he said and rubbed her hands. Miguel gave the best hand rubs but it wasn't enough.

"Can I have a hug?" she asked.

Miguel stood up.

"Come." He pulled Noelia in his arms.

His hugs were amazing. Her heartbeat had been off since the intense moment at Rubén's car. It felt as if she'd been drinking too much coffee. She couldn't sleep properly, constantly thinking of Rubén, which didn't improve the situation. Her left eye had started with that stupid twitch she got when she was stressed and it drove her crazy.

But Miguel's hug slowed down her heartbeat immediately. His hand on her back was so soothing, she could stay in his arms forever.

"Better?" he asked after she finally let go of him.

"Much better," she answered, pressing a kiss on his cheek. "Thank you, you really are the best! Why can't you be into women? I'd marry you on the spot."

Chapter Fifteen

Monday afternoon couldn't come fast enough. Noelia still hadn't found the solution to her problem but she couldn't wait to be with Rubén again. To see how things would develop.

The way he'd acted at the garden center and then afterward when they set up the vegetable garden together, had felt very intimate. It felt different.

Was there a tiny chance that she was more to him than just a game? That she wasn't only a dirty fantasy he was playing out?

When she entered his office, her heart was racing and her hands were sweaty but more than anything she felt happy and excited.

"Good afternoon Mr. Ramírez," she greeted him cheerfully.

She almost giggled, sticking to the set-up rules of addressing him by his last name in the office. She never realized that she was into role-playing until now. It was hot. *Very* hot.

"Close the door," he said.

The upset sound in his voice washed the smile off Noelia's face immediately. Wasn't he happy to see her?

She closed the door behind her and approached his desk. He was staring at her, his eyes cold.

What the fuck is going on? Did she do something? Or did she forget to clean something? She was 100% sure she emptied the garbage bin on Friday. And even if she didn't, there was no need to react like this.

"Why didn't you tell me?" he asked.

"Tell you what?"

"Stop pretending. I saw you."

"You saw what?" she asked.

"Yesterday. I saw you with your *boyfriend*."

The way he hissed "boyfriend" sounded so hateful. It took Noelia a moment to put two and two together.

He saw me yesterday? she wondered. With Miguel? He thought that Miguel was her boyfriend?

Noelia straightened her back and lifted her chin.

"Mr. Ramírez, I'm quite sure that informing you about my relationship status was *not* part of my work contract."

She didn't know where those words came from but she was right and glad she said it. She didn't like how he talked to her. What was he even thinking? First, he played his stupid games with her and now he got upset about her seeing someone else?

"If I had known I would not have -"

Noelia interrupted him.

"Not have what? Spanked me? Play your stupid games with me? Push your fancy butt plug into me and make me wear sexy maid outfits?"

This situation enraged her more and more. Maybe it was all the built-up frustration of the last weeks, but the words just kept on coming out.

"I'm not your toy Rubén. I'm also not a cleaning lady. I'm a math and physics teacher and I'm also a person who is fed up with your bullshit. So guess what? You can find yourself a new cleaning lady who's stupid enough to wear this outfit and clean up after you. I'm quitting!"

Chapter Sixteen

T he day was so hot that Noelia sweated even though she was naked in her house. Everyone else complained about the heat but she loved this about summer.

To sleep naked. Get up naked. Walk barefoot and never feel cold.

She sat on the sofa, reading a book and sipping on a can of coke.

When the doorbell rang she called, "Just one second!" and then raced up to her bedroom to grab some clothes. Still pulling the summer dress over her head she ran down the stairs to the front door.

It was Sunday.

Do they deliver packages even on Sundays now? she wondered.

She opened the door and froze.

Rubén.

He looked gorgeous as ever, dressed in some khaki shorts and a white T-shirt. He was very tanned, either from the gardening work or visiting the beach a lot.

"Hi," he said.

His voice stirred up the butterflies in her belly even more.

Three months. Three months without talking to him or

seeing him. Noelia had tried so hard to delete him and every-thing that happened out of her memory. She'd regretted overre-acting in his office and quitting before even hearing him out. Regretted not explaining to him that Miguel was a friend, not a boyfriend. But she'd been too proud to go back and apologize. After all, he was the one who had behaved like an idiot.

"Hi," she answered after digesting the initial shock of seeing him.

"I brought you some vegetables. You've helped me plant them, so I really wanted you to try them."

Noelia only noticed now that he held a huge basket filled with vegetables in all colors. There were yellow peppers, red peppers, cucumbers, tomatoes, zucchini, swiss chard, lettuce, and herbs sticking out.

"Thank you," she answered. "But how am I supposed to eat all of this?"

"I-. I also came to apologize," he said. His eyes met hers, making Noelia feel faint. "I'm very sorry, Noelia. How I treated you wasn't right. I would have *never* touched you if I'd known that you were with someone else. I just felt like there was something between us. I mean-. You did ask me to discipline you? *Twice.* I just hope you didn't feel like I forced you into something that you didn't want to do?"

Forced me into something I didn't want?

The pictures of Rubén spanking her in his living room as well as in his office, immediately passed in front of her eyes. She'd wanted it. She'd wanted it all and so much more.

"The only thing that wasn't right was how you reacted after seeing me with another man. Why Rubén? Why were you so angry that day?"

She'd been wanting to know this for so long.

"Isn't that obvious?" he asked.

"No, it's not, but you will explain it to me."

Noelia put her hands on her hips and lifted her chin. When she wanted to, she was perfectly capable of showing her dominant side as well. All her students knew this and did not dare to test out her patience.

"I was jealous. I had hoped you were mine. That you would be mine. And then I realized that this was all in my head. Some crazy fantasy I made up, imagining there was something between us." Rubén looked down at the vegetables for a second and then back at Noelia. "Like I said, I'm very sorry."

"Okay then. Apology accepted. Would you like to come inside?"

It took her a lot of concentration to act all cool, calm, and collected, when in reality she felt like jumping and screaming.

"No, no, no, I don't want to cause you any more trouble," he said.

"At least help me bring this huge basket to the kitchen."

Noelia saw his hesitation but she didn't give him a choice. She walked inside the house, holding the door open for him to follow her. Then she shut the door behind Rubén, with no intention of letting him leave her house ever again.

Chapter Seventeen

"I 'm also sorry," she said while taking the vegetables out of the basket and putting them on a big platter.

"What for? You didn't do anything wrong."

"Well-. I think I overreacted a little bit. And I'm sorry because I didn't even try to explain to you that the guy you saw me with wasn't my boyfriend."

Noelia looked at Rubén who's expression switched to confusion.

"But then who was the guy?" he asked.

"Miguel. My best friend. My *gay* best friend."

Rubén's gaze was so intense that Noelia felt hot all of a sudden. She held her breath as he stepped closer to her. He was so close now that she needed to lift her head to continue looking into his eyes. His sparkling beautiful eyes stirred up wanting, needing, and lust inside of her.

"No boyfriend?" he asked?

"No boyfriend," she answered, biting her lip.

"No boyfriend stopping me from doing dirty things to you?"

She shook her head.

"No boyfriend interfering with me spanking you?"

"No boyfriend," she repeated as she felt the wetness of her pussy slowly running down the insides of her thighs.

Rubén stepped even closer, pushing Noelia against her kitchen counter. She was trapped between his arms. His muscular thigh squeezed in between her legs and the pressure of it against her needy cunt felt so good that she needed all her willpower to not start rubbing herself on him.

Could he feel the heat? Would she stain his nice khaki pants?

"No boyfriend stopping me from kissing you?"

His mouth was so close to hers that she felt his breath. Her lips were tingling.

She couldn't wait any longer. She couldn't wait any other second. Couldn't and didn't want to. Determined, she moved forward to close the gap but Rubén moved backward.

Stop playing with me, she thought.

His hand wrapped around the back of her neck, his fingers intertwining in her hair. And then he claimed her mouth. Possessive and rough. His kiss took her breath away and the pressure of his leg between her thighs wasn't the only thing getting harder.

She willingly opened her mouth, letting him explore her while she gave in, rubbing herself on his thigh.

Not letting go of her, his free hand slid down and slowly moved up her summer dress. Rubén abruptly stopped kissing her. The surprise of finding her completely naked under the dress was written all over his face. He stared down at her uncovered pussy.

Noelia was grinning. Startling Mr. Rubén Ramírez Armengol seemed like a great achievement.

"Do you think it's appropriate to open your door to strangers, wearing nothing but a dress?" he asked.

"You're not a stranger."

"You didn't know it was me."

"True."

"So?"

"So what?"

"Do you think it's appropriate?"

"Probably not."

"Probably not?" He raised his eyebrows.

"No it's not," she answered, trying to hold back the giggle that wanted to come out but without success.

"Ms. Garrido, I believe this is the second time that I have to discipline you for not wearing any underwear under your dress."

"Yes, Mr. Ramírez."

"Where's your bedroom?" he asked.

"Upstairs, why?"

Rubén didn't answer.

Noelia screamed when he suddenly manhandled her over his shoulder. She didn't dare to move or kick out of fear he could accidentally drop her. Her head was banging against his back while her butt was fully exposed over his shoulder. It was uncomfortable and scary being carried up the stairs like that.

Only once they arrived in her bedroom, she started fighting him. A sharp slap of his hand landed on her ass before he maneuvered her onto the bed.

Noelia fell on her back with Rubén on top of her. He grabbed her wrists to hold her down and kissed her again. His knee pushed right between her legs.

Is this an invitation to rub herself on it? Even if not, she couldn't resist pressing herself against him, lifting her hips for some needed relief.

The kiss was rough and full of passion. They both wanted more and couldn't wait any longer. Three months without seeing each other had been way too long.

"Please fuck me Rubén," Noelia begged. She needed more. Her cunt needed more than a knee to rub on. And she wanted to feel him inside of her. As close as possible.

"First things first," he answered and pulled her up and over his lap. "Did you really think I'd forget?" he asked as he started spanking her gently.

Her dress was tangled around her waist, exposing every inch

of her naked butt in front of him. Rubén took his time spanking her, making her ass jiggle again and again and again. Noelia smiled and got comfortable over his lap. She wasn't embarrassed this time. She didn't feel shy. She was just horny beyond belief and couldn't be happier at this very moment.

Slowly but surely he built up the heat, spanking her harder as the time passed by. Her butt tingled when he stopped.

"Spread your legs," he demanded. His voice had that strict tone which made her wet and excited every time she heard him speak like this.

Noelia did as told, spreading her thighs as much as she could in this position. Now, not only her bottom tingled from the spanking but also her pussy because she could feel his eyes on her. Looking at her. Examining her.

Can he see how wet he makes me?

The touch of his finger, painting along the line of her slit made her moan.

It was the very first time he touched her pussy and she wanted more. Instinctively she spread her legs wider.

Rubén continued. His fingers touched her so lightly, that she wondered if she was maybe just imagining it. He explored the outside of her pussy and then gently rubbed her clit.

Noelia held her breath, indulging in his soft touch.

SLAP. SLAP. SLAP. SLAP.

The sudden switch from her clit getting rubbed to her ass being spanked again was completely unexpected. Noelia protectively closed her legs only to have them pushed apart again by Rubén before he continued spanking her.

His slaps were more intense than before but the feeling was absolutely amazing. Every smack shook her butt and intensified the throbbing in her pussy. Noelia enjoyed every minute of her sweet punishment for opening the door without wearing any underwear.

"Get up," he said.

She pushed herself up from his lap. Rubén opened his khaki

CHAPTER SEVENTEEN

shorts and freed his very hard and very gorgeous cock. He watched her and without saying anything, she knew what he wanted and she wanted the same.

Eagerly she bent down, grabbed his dick, and guided it to her lips. His cock felt hot and powerful in her hand. Softly she kissed the tip of it. Then she wet her lips before kissing it again, with her mouth slightly opened. She licked the almond-shaped tip, enjoying the smooth feeling of it. Noelia looked up to Rubén and he nodded.

She moved her hand up and down his shaft while watching him to see his reaction. His intense gaze turned glossier with each stroke so she decided to combine her hands and mouth. She moistened her lips again and then as she stroked down his cock she took his tip in her mouth. Each time her hand moved down, her mouth followed, taking in a little more of Rubén's dick. Noelia moved slowly at first but once she couldn't go any deeper she started thrusting faster, her lips wrapped tightly around him.

Rubén's breathing got faster as well. His arousal turned her on even more. She loved sucking him and pleasing him. If he already felt so amazing in her mouth, how great would his hard cock feel inside her pussy?

"Stop," he said and pushed her head gently away from his dick.

As soon as he wasn't in her mouth anymore, Noelia felt herself pulled back over his knees.

"Time for your second round of spanking."

A second round? she wondered.

There was no gentle warm-up this time. Round two was a firm, no-nonsense spanking that took her breath away. His hand flew down on her butt nonstop now. Noelia went from holding her breath to huffing and puffing and back to holding her breath again.

He had only really just started on round two and she was already having a hard time holding still for her punishment.

SLAP. SLAP. SLAP. SLAP.

Noelia squirmed on Rubén's lap, moving her hips from side to side.

"Don't. Move," he said.

Noelia took a deep breath and concentrated on staying still on his lap but her resolution was quickly thrown overboard as he continued his punishment, smacking her backside without mercy.

SLAP. SLAP. SLAP. SLAP.

If it weren't for Rubén holding on to her, she would have fallen off his lap from squirming so much.

"I told you, don't move," he repeated.

His right leg lifted and locked in both of her legs. Unable to move now, there was no more escaping. No squirming. No kicking.

Slap after slap landed where they were supposed to, coloring her backside crimson red. Noelia grunted and moaned while gasping for air. In an attempt to protect her sore butt, her hand flew back, only to be caught by Rubén. His fingers intertwined with hers, locking her hand in the small of her back.

Holding his hand felt good. He squeezed her hand and that was all the support she needed.

Another minute passed by and then he finally stopped, moved his leg lock off her, and helped her to get off his knees. Noelia was out of breath but Rubén's hard cock caught her eyes immediately.

"Yes. You may continue now," he said.

Wow. This man is so dirty, she thought.

So perfect. It felt as if he knew all her secret fantasies.

Chapter Eighteen

Noelia bent down to take his cock back into her mouth. The hot, burning feeling of her ass and the memory of what he'd just done to her, made her suck him even deeper.

She wanted to be the best he ever had. To impress him and satisfy him, so that he would get addicted to her and never let her go again.

"Stop. Get on top of me," he said.

Rubén lay down on the bed and Noelia climbed on top of his legs.

"The other way around."

"The other way around?" Noelia asked.

"Yes. I want to taste your pussy, Noelia. I've been fantasizing about it since the day I met you."

He's been fantasizing about tasting my pussy since that day?

She suddenly felt shy about it. About him seeing her pussy this close up in bright daylight. About him tasting her. What if he didn't like her taste?

"Get your pussy in my face right now or I'll continue spanking you."

More spanking? No, thank you. Her butt had definitely had enough.

It felt awkward but she turned around as told and slowly lowered herself down over his head with her legs spread. Rubén instantly wrapped his hands around her thighs and pulled her further down until his tongue slid along her pussy. The sensation was so intense, that a moan escaped Noelia.

Rubén's gorgeous cock twitched right in front of her. She didn't hesitate this time. She continued sucking Rubén's cock while enjoying his tongue doing magic on her clit.

Her spit was all over his dick and dripping down. It was so nice and slippery that it was easy to slide him deep inside her throat in this position. The angle was just perfect. The only issue was that she had a hard time concentrating on giving a great blowjob while being so distracted by what Rubén's mouth did to her.

Noelia took a break to fully enjoy it. She stopped moving but still had Rubén's dick deep in her throat. It felt amazing. His cock muffled her moans while she indulged in his tongue driving her crazy.

A little smack on her ass reminded her to continue but all it did was turn her on even more. She lifted her head up and down once, only to indulge again in the intense twists and turns of his tongue playing with her clit.

When Rubén's hands spread her sore butt cheeks and his finger rubbed her tight bootyhole on top of it all, Noelia couldn't hold back anymore.

Her legs started shaking, as she pressed her pussy hard on Rubén's mouth, riding back and forth. Despite the thick cock in her mouth, Noelia's moans echoed loudly in the bedroom.

One of Rubén's arms wrapped around her lower back and pulled her body tightly against him. His passionate hug prolonged the waves rushing through her body over and over again. Bound by Rubén, she came long and hard.

When he let go of her she rolled over sideways onto the bed. She was out of breath and grinning like a crazy person.

"Are you tired already?" he asked.

"Just catching my breath."

"Good, because I would *really* like to fuck you now!"

Her grinning only grew wider.

"Excuse me, Sir, is this how they speak in the suburbs?"

"Are you trying to provoke me again?"

She turned to pull a condom out of her night table and threw it at Rubén.

"I see. Always prepared," he said, raising his eyebrows.

She could see that he wasn't happy.

"Just shut up and fuck me already."

Noelia couldn't tell where was up or down. Within a second she found herself back over Rubén's lap, and his hand smacking her butt.

"You better watch your language," he scolded her.

"Ow!" she squeaked. "You better stop being so jealous then!"

Noelia laughed and then screamed again. "No need to flip out just because I have condoms in the house!"

"I can't hear your apology."

Rubén gave her another hard slap.

"Okay okay, I'm sorry!"

His hand firmly rubbed her bottom for a moment.

"Now get on your hands and knees and hand me another condom," he said.

"What happened to the one I gave you?"

"You mean the one *you threw* at me?"

Noelia giggled again and Rubén smirked as well.

"Give me another condom unless you want to end up over my lap for round four."

She hurried up pulling out a new condom from the night table and then got on her hands and knees.

There was definitely no need for another spanking. Her butt would be sore enough.

· · ·

Feeling Rubén's thick cock spreading her swollen lips and pushing inside her cunt bit by bit was the best feeling of her life.

If only time could stand still.

How many times had she fantasized about him fucking her? And now it was actually happening.

He moved slowly until he was all the way in and his loins pushed against her. She felt his balls against her ass.

So good.

So, so good.

Rubén stayed still for a moment, letting her pussy adjust to his width. The only thing that moved was his dick twitching inside of her. When he started thrusting slowly in and out of her, Noelia let her moans out freely. She was in seventh heaven.

"You are so beautiful," he said behind her.

Rubén slowly built up momentum, pushing harder and harder inside of her. His speed picked up until his loins smacked loudly against her bottom.

Noelia switched from her hands down to her elbows and arched her back. This felt even better. His cock now hit her in just the right spot. It felt amazing how he claimed her. How he made her his, using her for his pleasure.

Rubén went on and on and on. This man truly had stamina, giving her such a long and hard pounding.

"Turn Noelia, let me make love to you."

He pulled out completely and gently pushed on her hip to make her fall over to the side.

Did he really just say that? she wondered. The arrogant notary who enjoyed dominating his cleaning lady wanted to make love?

Noelia turned on her back and spread her legs to make space for him. Rubén grabbed her hands and his fingers intertwined with hers. Their eyes locked as he slid inside of her, closing the space between them.

When he lowered his lips to hers, kissing her softly and gently, the heat spread all over her body. Noelia felt lighthearted.

Responding to his kiss, she tilted her hips. And then he started moving slowly.

The contrast to the pounding before couldn't be more extreme. She loved his weight on her, his hair tickling her body.

Noelia needed his closeness. She needed to inhale his smell and watch his face while he made love to her. She was scared that if she closed her eyes, he might disappear and that everything turned out to be just a dream.

"I think I'm in love with you," she said.

The words just slipped out but she didn't care. She needed to say it, even if he didn't feel the same. There was no point in trying to keep this a secret any longer. If she was honest with herself, she'd loved him from the moment she met him.

Loved him and hated him.

Who would have thought these feelings were so closely related? Both strong and passionate.

Rubén smiled at her. Did he find it funny that she just openly confessed her feelings?

"I'm in love with you too Noelia. And I've been in love with you for a long time already."

She took a deep breath, not having realized that she held it all this time waiting for his reaction.

He kissed her before he started moving again.

Noelia wrapped her legs around his waist and Rubén thrusted inside of her. Again and again, until they both let go.

He loves me.

He's loved me for a long time.

Epilogue

Noelia's heart was pounding excitedly. What better way to celebrate their first wedding anniversary than with a reminder of how it had all started?

She knew Rubén would be home any minute now. Carefully, she'd tipped over the plant pot in their home office, making sure the earth was spread out everywhere.

It was a mess. A huge mess she'd have to clean up eventually but it would be well worth it.

Maybe it was the excitement of what he would possibly do to her or of the butt plug twisting in her ass. She was so aroused already, that she knew she'd come in no time today.

Her pussy twitched when she heard the key in the door. Noelia couldn't wait to see his face.

Rubén stared at her. His eyes turned glossy instantly, taking in her cleaning lady outfit. Then he saw the earth thrown all over the floor.

Surprise succeeded, she thought.

And he didn't even know yet that she was wearing the butt plug.

"I'm so sorry Mr. Ramírez. I will clean this up right away."

Rubén closed the distance between them and towered over Noelia, his hands crossed in front of his chest. He'd found his composure quicker than she'd expected and naturally slipped into his dominant role.

"Do you know what happens to cleaning ladies who create more dirt than they actually clean up, Ms. Garrido?"

His voice was so stern, that Noelia felt like she was actually in real trouble.

"No Sir."

"They get the dirty treatment, Ms. Garrido. The *very* dirty treatment. You know what I mean, don't you?"

"Yes Sir."

"Stay here, I'll be right back."

And back he was, with the cane in hand.

Noelia bit her lip. The sight of the cane made her equally nervous and aroused. The sting could feel so good but could also hurt a lot. Chances were, that Rubén made her feel both qualities of it today.

"Put your hands on the desk and stick your butt out."

Noelia followed his instructions and felt Rubén lifting her dress to her waist. He proceeded to pull down her white full-backs, leaving them hanging at the height of her knees.

A slight tug on her butt plug confirmed that he'd noticed her second surprise of the evening.

"Make sure to look at the mess you've made while you take your punishment," he said.

"Yes Sir."

He stood next to her, putting his hand on her lower back. His hand was warm and reassuring. Then the tapping started.

Up and down, the cane covered every tiny bit of her butt and thighs. The feeling was good, like a massage. Especially when it smacked down close to her pussy, it felt amazing. She wanted to relax, indulge in this sensation, and endeavor every moment but she knew-

Even though she'd expected it, she squeaked and moved forward when the cane suddenly pulled through, leaving its first mark.

"Stick your butt out," he said, his voice firm.

The tapping continued, gently massaging her thighs and buttocks. Noelia loved every bit of it. And then Rubén pulled through again, leaving another red stripe below the last.

Noelia moaned but stayed put. A few more light taps and then another biting sting of the cane landed on her backside.

He continued. It was his game. She loved and dreaded it at the same time. It fucking turned her on. It was what she needed.

Rubén gave her everything she needed and then a tad more. He was her husband. The love of her life. A combination of the most sensitive man she knew with a dominant side that made her pussy dripping wet just thinking of it. He knew exactly how to push her boundaries.

"Put your hands back," he reminded her after her hands moved to the edge of his desk.

Back in position, he didn't give her a break this time.

One strike.

Two strikes.

Three strikes.

And then Noelia danced on her tippy toes rubbing her butt.

Rubén tapped the desk with the cane and she knew what he wanted. Quickly she assumed her position again. Not doing so would result in extras and she definitely wanted to avoid that.

She slowly exhaled when the light slaps wandered across her bottom again, letting her relax for a bit. Rubén went on and on. It was so good. He was so gentle. The tapping close to her pussy made her moan out loud. If she could rub herself on something right now, she would come right away.

Please don't stop, Noelia thought.

But he did.

"Look at this mess, Ms. Garrido. You will get ten strikes with the cane. There won't be any breaks. Stay in position or I will start all over again. Is that understood?"

Noelia's pussy throbbed. Noelia's pussy was always a traitor in these situations.

Ten strikes without moving? If not he will he start all over again?

She was sweating already thinking of it and yet her pussy didn't care. Her pussy loved Rubén. His threats. His stern voice. And the cane.

"Yes Sir," she answered.

She took a deep breath and clenched her teeth.

The first time the cane hit was okay. She was prepared. The second impact was harder. There was no break at all. The third strike made her grunt. The fourth made her forget to clench those teeth together and she moaned out loud.

Number five, six, and seven seemed to come down in the same spot right on the crease between her butt and thighs. The spot that made her moan in ecstasy if it were just light tapping but now it took her all her concentration to stay put. To not move, no matter how much it burned.

She was relieved when the cane wandered further down its route. Eight.

Two more. Just two more.

Noelia cried out when number nine hit hard and then the tenth followed, accompanied by a high-pitched scream.

It was over. Her punishment was over leaving her butt on fire.

The weird thing was that as soon as it was over, she craved more. It was always like this. First, she wanted to get spanked. Then, when she got spanked she wanted it to be over as quickly as possible but as soon as Rubén was done with her, she already fantasized about the next time he would spank her.

Rubén opened a drawer of his desk. Even though Noelia really wanted to rub her stinging butt, she didn't move. She knew she wasn't supposed to move unless he'd instructed her to.

The lube dripped on her cheeks. It was cool and soothing. She closed her eyes and heard him opening his belt buckle.

. . .

Rubén's cock felt hot against her skin. He used his dick to spread the lube all over her ass, rubbing himself on her. As soon as her glowing backside was covered in glossy slipperiness, he moved on to her pussy. He rubbed himself on her swollen lips and then slapped his cock against her. Again and again.

Noelia was moaning. She stuck her butt out as much as possible and spread her legs wider to give him the best access possible.

When he tugged on her butt plug on top of it, she was already edging.

While he pulled on the plug, his dick pushed against her pussy. The mix of lube and her own wetness was so slippery that there was no resistance at all.

His tip slid right in and Noelia arched her back to take him in deeper. But Rubén held back. He continued playing with her plug. He pulled it to that sweet spot where she was fully stretched and held it there.

Noelia couldn't concentrate on anything else anymore. The sudden sensation of Rubén's cock pushing inside her wet cunt made her legs go weak. Both her pussy and her ass were stretched out to the max now.

Rubén stopped moving for a few seconds before pulling his dick back out slowly while pushing the plug deeply back inside of her.

Her pussy was throbbing, aching to be filled again, while her tight ass clenched around the thin stem of the stainless steel plug.

Again, she begged in her head but didn't dare to make demands or move.

Luckily Rubén seemed to think the same. His dick rested at the entrance of her pussy and his finger started pulling on the anal plug. Then his cock slid back inside her pussy bit by bit. The further he dug inside her needy cunt, the more his finger pulled on the plug, stretching out her ass slowly but surely.

The sensation was out of this world. The contrast. The intensity.

The tugging on the steel toy while Rubéns cock pushed inside her pussy. As if that wasn't enough, Rubén started twisting and turning the plug. Noelia's moaning was more of a whining now. This was the sweetest torture ever.

"Please, Sir. I need you to fuck me."

"I know exactly what you need. But you also know that the dirty treatment means that I will fuck your ass, not your pussy."

"Yes Sir," she answered.

Of course, she knew this. She wanted this. She loved his dick in her ass more than anything. If anyone would have told her three years ago that anal would become her favorite thing of all, she would have never believed it. But there was nothing more intense. Nothing that made her feel closer to Rubén than anal sex.

Rubén slowly pulled his cock out while simultaneously pulling on the plug this time. Right as his dick came out of her, he pulled a bit more on the plug and her ass opened up and released it.

Suddenly she was empty. No more plug stretching out her ass and no more dick stretching out her pussy.

More lube dripped on her ass.

It was just a second and then his rock-hard tip pushed against the tight entrance where the plug had just been a minute ago.

Noelia pushed slightly against his cock to relax her muscles and then she felt the tip slip in.

Her ass was ready and so was she. Rubén was careful, sliding inside of her very very slowly. She guided his speed, pushing her hips back when she could take him a tad deeper. It was crazy how his cock always felt so much longer sliding inside her booty than when he slid inside her pussy.

But she loved it. She loved every tiny bit of it.

Her booty hole was so much more sensitive and somehow it radiated right into her pussy, intensifying the throbbing sensation.

All the way in, she thought, impatient to feel his balls push against her.

When his loins touched her, he grabbed her hips and pulled her even closer to him.

For a moment, they just stayed like this, letting Noelia's tight ass adjust to being filled. She indulged in that incredible feeling of their bodies being connected, not able to get any closer to each other.

Then Rubén started moving. Slowly, very slowly, he trusted in and out of her. Noelia moaned deeply as she felt every nerve cell inside her ass perceptive of her husband's cock sliding in and out.

He kept the slow pace but pushed in deeply and with force just like she loved it.

"This, Ms. Garrido, is what dirty cleaning ladies get when they make a mess."

"Yes, Mr. Ramírez," Noelia gasped between moans.

"And you love it, don't you?"

"Yes Sir."

"Good. Because getting spanked and fucked by your boss is part of your contract, isn't it?"

"Yes, Mr. Ramírez."

"You're allowed to touch yourself now."

Noelia slipped her hand down between her legs. She'd been waiting for his permission. His permission to touch herself. His permission to come.

The mere push of her hands on her swollen pussy started the wave. Rubéns dick continued thrusting slowly and powerfully in and out of her while the sounds of her deep moans filled the room.

"That's it," he encouraged her. "Come for me."

Noelia's orgasm radiated from her ass to her pussy, wave after wave, lasting deliciously long. She was slowly calming down herself as she felt Rubéns cock expand, stretching her to the point where she thought she might burst, as he came inside her tight ass.

Still inside of her, Rubén hugged Noelia from the back and kissed her on the neck.

"Best anniversary surprise ever!" he said.

———

Thank you for reading *The Strict Notary*. If you're curious to find out what went on inside Rubén's head after he met Noelia, then head over to your free bonus chapter at:

https://annikastout.com/bonus

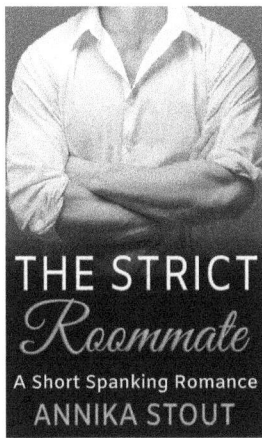

THE STRICT
Roommate
A Short Spanking Romance
ANNIKA STOUT

Two-Hour Short Read / Opposites Attract/ Spanking Level 2 / Spanking Implements: Hand/Hairbrush / NO Anal (bonus scene only)

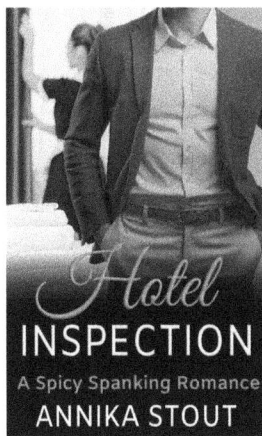

Hotel
INSPECTION
A Spicy Spanking Romance
ANNIKA STOUT

Two-Hour Short Read / Enemies-To-Lovers / Spanking Level 3 / Spanking Implements: Hand/Hairbrush / Anal Play

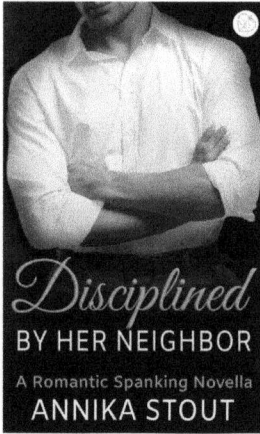

Disciplined
BY HER NEIGHBOR
A Romantic Spanking Novella
ANNIKA STOUT

Two-Hour Short Read / Enemies-To-Lovers / Neighbors-To-Lovers / Spanking Level 4 / Spanking Implements: Hand/Belt/Cane / Anal Play / MfM

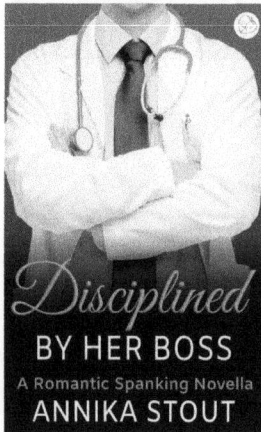

Disciplined
BY HER BOSS
A Romantic Spanking Novella
ANNIKA STOUT

Two-Hours Short Read / Workplace Romance / Spanking Level 3 / Spanking Implements: Hand/Ruler/Cane / Anal Play

About the Author

Annika Stout's relationship is a real-life spanking romance. Whenever she's not writing, she is most probably bent over Mr. Stout's knee to find more inspiration.

It wasn't always like that, it took her years to be confident enough to say what she wants and needs. She hopes that her books can help others do the same.

Annika offers contemporary spanking romance without the dark BDSM stuff. Just your typical guy next door, a hot boss or co-worker who isn't afraid to make a strong woman's fantasy come true.

Why not give one of Annika's books to your partner to introduce him/her to your kink? You can read it together or leave a note with it.

If you feel weird about it, just remember that spankos are considered vanillas within the BDSM community.

For more books and updates:
https://annikastout.com

instagram.com/authorannikastout
tiktok.com/@annikastout_author

Milton Keynes UK
Ingram Content Group UK Ltd.
UKHW022351060724
445042UK00001B/28